Magic Pony

Pet Rescue

Natty looked up and cried out with delight. Ned, the pony in the poster, was alive again. He leaned from her bedroom window as if over a stable door. She quickly looked round to make sure no one else was witness to this extraordinary sight.

"Ned, I'm so glad to see you. I've been wanting you to come back for ages."

Follow all of Natty and Ned's adventures!
Collect all the fantastic books in the
Magic Pony series:

Magic Pony

Pet Rescue

ELIZABETH LINDSAY
Illustrated by John Eastwood

■SCHOLASTIC

For Jessamy, with love.

Scholastic Children's Books,
Commonwealth House, 1–19 New Oxford Street,
London WC1A 1NU, UK
a division of Scholastic Ltd
London ~ New York ~ Toronto ~ Sydney ~ Auckland

First published in the UK by Scholastic Ltd, 1997
This edition published in the UK by Scholastic Ltd, 2004

Text copyright © Elizabeth Lindsay, 1997
Illustrations copyright © John Eastwood, 1997

ISBN 0 439 95962 4

Printed and bound by Nørhaven Paperback A/S, Denmark

2 4 6 8 10 9 7 5 3

Contents

Chapter 1
Visitors

Natty lay stretched out on her bed, hands behind her head, with her tabby cat, Tabitha, a purring ball on her chest. Drifting into a wonderful pretend, Natty imagined Ned, the chestnut pony in the poster on her wall, jumping from his picture.

– "Take me on an adventure, Ned," she said, climbing on to his strong back. "Like you did before!" With a whoosh and whirl of magic wind, they are in the field on the other side of the lane. Here Penelope Potter's *pony Pebbles watches in astonishment as they soar over a line of blue barrels, the very barrels Pebbles jumps so often with his owner. And Natty doesn't wobble once, for in a pretend everything goes according to plan and she never ever falls off.*

There was a big sigh and Natty opened her eyes, gently toppling Tabitha on to the duvet, before sitting up. Tabby curled into the warm space left behind and promptly fell asleep. Natty swung her feet to the floor, gazed at Ned's picture and sighed another sigh, one of loss and longing.

It seemed like for ever ago that she had bought the pony poster at Cosby's Magic Emporium.

A long, chestnut hair from Ned's tail hung on the wall above her bed. The hair wasn't pretend, it was real, and Natty knew in her heart of hearts that Ned could still come out of the poster – even if the magic had worked only once so far. Maybe, when Jamie next went to buy a magic trick, she should go too and ask Mr Cosby if she had to do something special to make the magic happen.

She stood up to touch the cool, shiny paper and ran a finger along Ned's white blaze.

"Are you going to come alive again? Are you?" she asked, but nothing changed and there was not the slightest hint that Ned was anything other than a pony in a picture.

Natty turned to her three china horses on the window-sill. Esmerelda had her back to Prince and Percy.

Now Natty rearranged them into a nose-to-nose huddle so they could talk to each other, unaware that the head in the poster had turned, just a little, to follow what she was doing.

"Esmerelda, Prince, Percy – I'm going on an adventure. Tell Ned to come too?" But the three china horses were silent.

It was no good. She would have to adventure on her own. Natty grabbed an invisible rein, jumped on to a chestnut back that wasn't there and set off at a canter to the top of the stairs. Then clumpity, clumpity, clumpity all the way down to the bottom, riding like the wind. Her thumping feet brought Mum hurrying from the living room.

"Natty, that's an awful lot of noise. I thought you'd fallen downstairs." Natty jogged on the spot; her pony prancing. "If you've got nothing better to do, Jamie's outside and might like some help. He's going to make Fred disappear."

Natty shook her head. "He'll never do it."

"I have my doubts too," admitted Mum. "But he insists on trying. Why don't you give him a hand?"

It was true that Jamie's conjuring was getting better and his latest card trick was brilliant. But he didn't stand a chance of making a goldfish vanish, let alone a goldfish in a bowl. No, she'd got better things to do than get involved with that.

"I'll just say hello to Pebbles," Natty said, and cantering to the front door, she reared up to undo the latch. "And Penelope if she's there." Mum smiled and left her to it.

Natty trotted down the garden path to the front gate. Ned would jump it with an easy leap and a swish of his tail. If she tried it, common sense told her she would end up flat on her face. If only he would come out of his poster.

Reaching the other side of the lane, Natty reined in her invisible pony and dismounted. She put her foot on the middle rung of the field gate, hoisted herself up and leaned over.

She was just in time to see Penelope lead Pebbles out of the far gate to his stable. Natty swung herself to the other side and, landing on her invisible pony's back, set off at a gallop across the well-cropped grass.

"Whoa boy, whoa," she said, arriving at the far gate. Breathing hard, she let herself into the small stable yard and set her pretend pony free.

"Hello, Penelope. Need any help?"

Penelope, who was tying Pebbles's halter rope to the string on the ring outside his stable, considered the offer.

"You can groom him if you like.
You can't ride him though. My
cousin Daisy's going to do that. I'm
getting him ready for her."

"Your cousin?" Natty enquired, eager to get her hands on a brush before Penelope changed her mind.

"Daisy, Auntie Peg and Uncle Ralph are staying for the weekend. They're back at the house. I've come over to get Pebbles ready. Daisy's younger than me so I'm looking after her."

"That's nice," said Natty, fetching Pebbles's red-bristled dandy brush, ready to start. Penelope held up the pony's yellow stained tail and wrinkled her nose.

"It'll have to be washed, Pebbles.

Daisy can't ride you with a tail like that."

"Not a good idea," agreed Natty, happily, for if Penelope was busy tail-washing it meant she could brush away to her heart's content. She began at once on the pony's dappled grey neck. Pebbles stood like a rock with eyes half closed.

He was particularly itchy around the ears and when Natty scratched them he leaned into her hand and wobbled his bottom lip. She scratched harder. Wobble, wobble, wobble went the lip.

In the end Natty's fingers ached so much she had to stop and Pebbles was heard to breathe a sigh of regret.

She brushed his neck, his back, his tummy, his front and rear legs – and that was just one side. By the time Penelope arrived with a bucket of hot water, Natty was dust-covered and puffed.

"Not bad," said Penelope. "You've missed a bit there though, and don't forget to comb his mane."

Natty nearly said, And what did your last slave die of? but stopped herself. She didn't want to fall out with Penelope, not when she was to be allowed a go with the mane comb. She changed sides and brushed and brushed, while Penelope plunged the dirty tail into the hot water. Pebbles was quite

used to all this and carried on dozing, not minding at all when Penelope squeezed on a large dollop of horse shampoo and got down to a thorough rubbing. Soon his tail was a mass of dirty brown foam.

"Fill a bucket, Natty. I need to rinse it."

Natty put down the dandy brush and surveyed her work. Only the mane to do. But first, Madam Penelope wanted water. Honestly! Hadn't she heard of the word please?

Natty staggered back from the tap with a bucketful, only to be told to get another.

"I need loads," said Penelope. "To get all the soap out."

Dutifully, Natty filled another bucket. She was about to rummage in the grooming box for the mane comb when a car reversed down Penelope's drive, across the lane and into the little yard.

"Here they are," cried Penelope, whirling the dripping tail round and round and showering Natty.

"Hey, do you mind!"

"Natty, get rid of the buckets," Penelope ordered, thrusting two at her. "I'll quickly do his mane."

"But I was going to do that!"

Penelope ignored her.

Fed up, Natty dumped the buckets in the tack room. There wasn't much point in hanging about only to be in the way, so she started for the gate.

A girl, with a mass of blonde curls and wearing a new pair of jodhpurs and gleaming jodhpur boots, climbed from the car. Must be Daisy, thought Natty, and she watched from the top of the gate, envying the little girl her smart new riding clothes.

The man – Uncle Ralph, Natty supposed – opened the back of the car and revealed a brown hutch.

"Get the other end, Daisy."

"It's too heavy by myself," said Daisy.

Penelope glanced at Natty. Natty took the hint.

"I'll help," she said, jumping from her perch.

Daisy and Natty got one end and Uncle Ralph the other and between them they lifted out the hutch. They were about to place it on the concrete when the hutch door swung open.

"Careful, Flopper will get out," said Daisy.

But, as Natty realized on closer inspection, whoever or whatever Flopper was, he had already got out, for the hutch was empty.

Chapter 2
The Face at the Window

Natty quickly learned that Flopper was Daisy's pet rabbit. The most perfect, snow white creature in the whole world, with a name to match his ears.

"They flop sideways," sobbed Daisy, twisting Flopper's red lead in her hands. "And his paws are pink and his nose is pink and it twitches. You'll know him the moment you see him." But since Flopper appeared gone for ever, Daisy's sobs became heartbroken wails.

Daisy and her parents had arrived late yesterday evening, Natty was told. It had been too dark to find a place out of doors for Flopper to spend the night, so they had left him in the back of the car, locked in his hutch – or so they thought. Uncle Ralph had left a gap in the back door to make sure Flopper had plenty of fresh air.

But now, when they wanted to take him for a walk in Pebbles's field, he was gone, already walking himself goodness knows where.

Penelope clasped her hands over her ears, trying to cut out Daisy's agonizing cries.

"I'll look for him," said Natty, understanding that if Flopper were her pet rabbit she would be feeling just like Daisy.

"Look anywhere you like," said Penelope. "But a rabbit on its own all night in our garden will certainly have been eaten by the fox."

Daisy's cries became instantly worse and Uncle Ralph looked even more worried. Natty thought it best not to mention that Tabitha had also been known to bring home the occasional rabbit. Instead, she tried to be of comfort.

"He may have found a nice little hole to hide in. He may have gone visiting and met up with other rabbits." At this crumb of hope, Daisy's wails lessened.

"Do you think so?" she asked, between sobs.

"It's possible."

Uncle Ralph sent Natty a grateful look.

"Anyway," said Natty. "I'll get going. I'll look in the lane, in Mrs Plumley's front garden, in ours and in the wood."

"Where will we look, Penelope?" Daisy asked, looking brighter now that positive action was to be taken.

"Our garden and the field, I suppose." Penelope sighed. "Both are huge; it'll take ages."

Natty waved goodbye. Her search would start straight away. She hurried past Uncle Ralph's shiny car and once out of sight, jumped upon her invisible pony and trotted into the lane. She looked this way and that. No white rabbit was to be seen.

Turning towards home, Natty reached next door's house first. She peered over the garden gate.

Nothing on the grass. Not a glimmer of white fur amongst Mrs Plumley's prize dahlias or behind the willowy hollyhocks. At the next gate, her own, a soft burbling sound, the sort horses make by blowing through their noses, brought her to an abrupt stop.

"Hello, down there!"

Natty looked up and cried out with delight. Ned, the pony in the poster, was alive again. He leaned from her bedroom window as if over a stable door. She quickly looked round to make sure no one else was witness to this extraordinary sight.

"Ned, I'm so glad to see you. I've been wanting you to come back for ages."

"Well, here I am," said the pony and promptly disappeared.

It wasn't until Natty saw a branch sway on the fig tree growing by the wall that she saw him again. Now as tiny as Percy, the smallest of her china horses, Ned sprang from leaf to leaf all the way down the tree until he balanced level with her nose.

"Help me down then and we'll go for a ride." His little voice reminded her of tinkling bells.

"A ride! Oh, Ned, I'd love to, but I'm looking for a lost rabbit."

"A lost rabbit, eh? I'll help you look."

With glowing eyes, Natty reached up two flat palms for Ned to climb on to, then carefully lowered him to the ground.

In the time it takes to blink, he
was at her side, big and strong, the
size Pebbles had been when she'd
groomed him, wearing a bridle
and a saddle, ready for
her to mount.

Natty took hold of the reins and swung herself on to his back. The moment her seat touched the saddle, sweatshirt, jeans and trainers were gone. In their place was a hacking jacket, jodhpurs and brown boots; underneath the jacket a shirt and tie. Her hands wore pale riding gloves and on her head was a velvet hard hat.

"I love the riding clothes! I could be Penelope Potter going to a horse show!" she exclaimed.

"You could indeed," said Ned, and he pulled the gate open with his teeth and went into the lane.

"Now where shall we look?"

"In Winchway Wood. It's this way. Turn left." Ned did so. "The rabbit's called Flopper and is completely white. He escaped in Penelope's garden."

Ned snorted and his trotting feet made delicate clicks on the road's hard surface; for, unlike Pebbles, he wore no shoes. It was strange not to hear the ring of metal.

Natty did her best up-down, up-down rising trot until they reached the path that led into the wood where the lane ended.

"Be careful, Ned. Lots of people walk their dogs this way. We mustn't be seen!"

"Don't worry. Just say hello and on we'll go."

"But you're a secret!"

"Where I come from is a secret. That you and I can become tiny is a secret. When we're ordinary like this, it doesn't matter so long as no one recognizes who you are."

"But they might."

"Dressed like that you have the perfect disguise. And, of course, I shall never speak when someone is near!" Ned's confidence in the riding clothes as a disguise made Natty long to look at herself in the mirror. She pulled her chin-strap straight and sat tall, feeling a different person.

"Hold on tight," said Ned. "And keep a lookout for that bunny."

Natty twisted some mane around her fingers just in case and Ned broke into a canter. To her delight, Natty found she hardly wobbled at all.

"You're getting better," cried Ned. "I told you I'd teach you to ride. Do you remember?" Natty did remember. "Don't you worry about a thing. Relax and it's as easy as breathing. You can leave the steering to me."

Natty did just that, enjoying herself utterly, her eyes darting here and there, ever on the lookout for a white rabbit. Ned cantered beneath the stately beech trees, his hooves beating out a steady rhythm on the path. A log lay ahead and Natty knew he was going to jump it.

"Don't worry, you'll hardly notice we've left the ground," Ned cried. The log came closer and the nearer they got the bigger it looked, but Ned made nothing of it. They flew over it and Natty stayed on even when they thudded to the ground on the other side.

A bubble of laughter burst from
her. Jumping was fun.

Now Ned galloped, ears flat back, his mane flying, while the wind forced tears from Natty's eyes and whistled in her ears.

Then suddenly there was a dog, small and white, barking ferociously.

It came at them without warning. Ned shied off the path, made a whiplash turn and raised a forefoot, ready to confront the foe. Natty landed halfway up his neck.

"It's Ruddles," she gasped, clinging on. "Sit, Ruddles! Sit and stay!"

The little dog stopped, cocked his head on one side and sat, wondering how this stranger knew his name. Natty hauled herself back into the saddle. "Ruddles lives next door." The little dog raised an ear and waited expectantly. "Mrs Plumley must be taking him for a walk. Look, here she comes."

Stout Mrs Plumley waddled down the path towards them, waving Ruddles's lead.

"Ruddles, come here you little varmint," she called. "You leave that pony alone."

"Let's go, Ned," said Natty. "If she recognizes me, she'll certainly tell Mum and then I'll have some explaining to do."

"I've already told you, you have the perfect disguise," said Ned. "It's a good time to try it out. But remember, if you get off, don't let go of the reins or the riding clothes'll vanish."

Natty crossed her fingers and wished for luck.

"Good dog, Ruddles. Good boy," said the old lady, puffing up and stooping to clip on the lead. She smiled up at Natty. "Sorry about

his barking, dear. He's a noisy so and so but he don't mean no harm." Natty smiled back but didn't say anything.

"You've got a pretty pony there. A lovely chestnut colour. What's his name?"

Natty swallowed nervously.

"Ned."

"What's that you say?" Mrs Plumley tipped her head to one side and waited.

"He's called Ned!"

"And a right handsome Ned he is too," said Mrs Plumley, patting Ned's sleek neck. "Well, I must be getting on. Come along, Ruddles. Enjoy your ride, me dear."

"Thank you," said Natty. "I will." And she breathed a huge sigh of relief as Mrs Plumley pulled the reluctant Ruddles on down the path.

"There," said Ned. "It's just as I said."

"It is," said Natty, grinning hugely.

"It's a real disguise."

Ned raised his head and stepped out in a businesslike way.

"Let's get on with this search," he said. "We've got a white rabbit to find."

Chapter 3
Rabbit Search

Ned trotted between the trees, twisting round the solid trunks. Natty scanned the ground at either side while Ned kept a forward lookout. From grassy patches the grey wood-dwelling rabbits hurried and scurried, flashing bobtails as they hid down holes and disappeared between tree roots. But a snow white rabbit with pink nose and paws was nowhere to be seen.

For all their looking hither and thither, Natty and Ned could only reach one conclusion – Flopper was not in Winchway Wood.

"Well, you can't say we haven't looked," said Natty. "We must have covered every bump, dip, nook and cranny."

"We certainly have." Ned came to a stop and blew a burbling pony sigh. "It's been a good ride but I say we go home."

Ned turned for the path and Natty was filled with a certain sadness. She loved being on Ned's strong back; already he was a real friend. But she was concerned for Flopper.

"I hope Penelope was wrong when she said a night out for Flopper meant the fox would get him."

Ned blew again, pursuing a thought. "He's found somewhere more rabbit-friendly, that's what he's done." And he stretched his long neck.

"What's more rabbit-friendly than a wood full of rabbits?" wondered Natty.

"A garden full of cabbages, lettuces and juicy peas!"

"Of course," said Natty. "Grass must be boring for a rabbit that's used to treats. I bet Daisy gives him lots."

"I'm sure she does," agreed Ned.

"Like Mrs Plumley gives Pebbles a carrot every day. He likes it so much he waits by the gate."

"There you are then."

"Well," said Natty. "The nearest place to Penelope's garden where a rabbit can find all those treats is our vegetable patch."

"Mmm! Better take a look," said Ned.

"But he can't get in. Dad knows all about rabbits. There's netting right round the whole garden." Natty drew her eyebrows together. "I keep thinking he might have gone the other way, to the main road, and got himself squashed by a passing car. That would be terrible."

"It certainly would be," agreed Ned, trotting forwards. "The sooner we find out what's happened to him the better. We'll search the garden next."

They reached the path and ahead of them lay the log. Ned cantered towards it. His jump was effortless, although his rider slipped sideways. He stopped so Natty could straighten up.

"It was going downhill," she said, excusing herself and adjusting her hat.

"You're doing very well, very well indeed for a first ride out of doors."

They continued along the path and out of the woods, reaching Natty's house in a matter of moments.

"We'd better go round by the side gate," she said, dismounting. "There's less chance of bumping into anyone." Keeping hold of the reins she twisted round to admire her smart jodhpurs and shiny jodhpur boots.

"It would be best if you carry me," said Ned.

Natty knew her wonderful clothes would disappear the moment she let go. She closed her eyes. . .

"One, two, three!" . . . and dropped the reins. When she opened them again, Ned and the riding clothes had disappeared and she was back in her grubby jeans, sweatshirt, and boring old trainers.

But she brightened up when the tiny Ned trotted round her toes and she bent down with both hands outstretched.

He jumped neatly on to her palms and she lifted him carefully. Keeping her hands steady, Natty pushed the gate open with her bottom and slipped down the path to the back garden.

The first person she saw was Jamie. His conjuring gear was spread higgledy-piggledy across the grass and he was balancing his magician's top hat on a finger and holding his magic wand aloft. The goldfish bowl was sitting on the little table from the living room and Fred, fluttering his fins, was staring out at the flowers.

"Abracadabra, vroom, vroom vanish!" Jamie spun the hat on to his head and twirled his cloak. Fred, bowl and table were enveloped in blackness while Jamie began some kind of awkward struggle.

"Natty, be my assistant and I can do it," said Jamie, catching sight of her.

"Do what?" Natty asked, although she knew the answer.

"Make Fred disappear. I can't do it on my own because of the water. Every time I try I tip the bowl."

He uncovered the goldfish who was swimming round and round in frantic haste.

"Poor Fred, you're scaring him," said Natty. "Anyway that's cheating. It's not magic if you've got to get someone else to do it for you."

"Of course it's not cheating. Conjuring is sleight of hand, illusion and all that. An assistant just helps. What have you got there?"

Natty had been carrying on this conversation with her hands held out.

"Oh, nothing." And indeed, when she looked there was nothing. She shook them out to show this was true and at the same time glanced round. Much to her surprise it was Ned who'd vanished, although Natty knew it had nothing to do with Jamie's conjuring. Ned was hiding.

There was a distracting bang, crash and yelp in the shed and Dad danced into the garden holding his thumb. Natty rushed to see what the matter was, along with Mum, who ran from the kitchen.

"What's happened?" they both asked. Dad puffed and blew and, in an effort not to say rude words, went red in the face.

"I think it's his thumb," said Natty.

"Must have hit it with the hammer," said Jamie.

Dad let out a groan of a breath. "You could say that!"

"Bad luck," said Mum, gently lifting his hand to look. "Best run cold water on it to stop the bruising."

Natty leaned her face against Dad's arm. "Poor Dad. I hope it doesn't hurt too much."

"At least your thumb's still there," said Jamie, cheerily.

Dad ignored that remark and went indoors.

"Okay, you two, it's teatime," said Mum. "Stop what you're doing and come in. And don't leave that fish outside in case the cat gets it."

"Natty, can you bring Fred?" Jamie asked, dropping his cloak and hat in a pile and offering the bowl expectantly.

"Why can't you?" grumbled Natty.

"I need two hands for the table." Natty took the bowl, taking care not to slop any water, and peered at Fred. He seemed calmer now he'd stopped being shaken about, and he peered back.

Having to go in for tea was a real nuisance. Natty wanted to find Ned and look for Flopper. Fed up, she followed Jamie and the table indoors.

Natty was glad to get Fred safely back in his place on the bookshelf and, while Mum came in with a plate of sandwiches, she took a quick look out of the window. She hoped that Ned, wherever he was, realized she had been dragged in for tea.

Mum returned to the kitchen to collect the teapot.

"Natty, there's a cake on the side. Come and fetch it for me, will you?"

Having got as far as the kitchen, Natty was tempted to sneak outside but when she saw that the cake was a yummy chocolate one she carried it into the living room.

"When did you make this?" she asked.

"I didn't. Mrs Plumley did. It's a thank-you for keeping an eye on things while she's away."

"But she's not away."

"She will be tomorrow. She and Ruddles are going to town to stay with her sister for a few days."

"After tea I'll cut her a couple of lettuces and pull her some carrots to take," said Dad.

"She'd appreciate that," nodded Mum. "Carrots you buy never taste as good as the home-grown ones. Plates, Natty. Pass Dad a sandwich, Jamie." Natty gave Dad a plate and Jamie obediently offered the sandwiches.

"Wow, your thumb's going yuck red. I bet the nail comes off."

"Don't sound so excited," said Dad.

"What were you doing anyway?" Mum asked.

"There's a hole to mend. Some animal's pushed its way through the fence."

A hole in the fence! Natty's mind raced. Did that mean that Flopper was in the garden after all? She wished Mum would get on and cut the cake. She wanted to go and look.

"Now Jamie, tell me. . ." asked

Mum, sipping her tea and taking ages to get to the point. Natty fiddled impatiently with a sandwich. "Did you make Fred disappear?"

Jamie's face took on a look of despair.

"I need a rabbit. You can't do conjuring with a goldfish. The water tips out. Every magician should have a rabbit."

"And white doves," added Natty. "To pull from sleeves and top hats."

"Don't encourage him," said Mum. "A cat and a goldfish are plenty enough pets for one family."

"Don't even think of a rabbit," joined in Dad. "Garden pests, they are."

Natty fidgeted in her chair, aware that Flopper might be being a garden pest right now. Jamie scowled with disappointment.

At last Mum slid a knife through the gooey chocolate cake.

"Pass your plate, Natty."

Natty bit into the dark stickiness, lumpy with chocolate chips and gooey with cocoa cream filling.

It was bliss. She chewed quickly to the last mouthful when a loud whinny from the garden startled her into action. Ignoring the protests from Mum and Dad, she swallowed, plonked down her plate and ran.

It was Ned calling; she had to go.

Chapter 4
The Thief in the Garden

Natty charged out of the back door and raced down the path. Was she looking for a big Ned or a little Ned? She didn't know. When she got to the shed she found the big Ned behind it, tacked up and waiting. She knew what to do. She reached for his withers and vaulted.

"Well done," said the pony, and the moment she was astride a wild wind spun them away, leaving his voice an echo. When it was calm again it seemed as if they were in a different place. The wooden wall beside them climbed forever and feet the size of cars thudded along the vast plain of the path.

Natty cried out and clung on, while Ned cantered towards the dark space beneath the shed's floor. The black soles of Jamie's trainers rose above them, smacking down to miss them by a hair's breadth.

Ned swung round and together they peered out. More giant feet arrived and Natty recognized Dad's boots.

"Which way did she go, Jamie?" Dad's voice boomed out.

"I don't know. But I bet she's chasing after Penelope Potter on Pebbles. She's only got to hear a horse and she's gone."

"She's a cheeky little so and so running off like that in the middle of tea. Still, while I'm out here I'll pull those carrots for Mrs Plumley. Fetch me a bag will you?"

The feet clumped slowly away in different directions.

"Sounds like I'm in trouble," said Natty.

"And so's that rabbit!" nodded Ned.

"Have you seen him?"

"No, but I've seen what he's eaten. Four lettuces munched down to stumps, enough carrot tops to feed a rabbit warren and chewed pea pods scattered everywhere."

As if to prove Ned's point an outraged cry rose from the vegetable patch as Dad discovered the damage.

"How do you know it was Flopper?"

"I found a hole in the fence with tell-tale hairs sticking to the wire. Something white and furry has squeezed through all right."

"At least he's safe," said Natty. "Even if he is going to be the most unpopular rabbit in the universe when Dad finds out it was him."

Ned snorted.

"And the fattest."

"Where shall we look?" Natty asked. "We must find him before he does any more damage."

"I've looked everywhere," said Ned. "Up the runner beans, around the beetroot, between the onions. You name it, I've been there."

"Maybe he's gone to lie down," said Natty.

"I wouldn't be at all surprised."

"Or set off to find his nice cosy hutch."

"To do that he'll have had to squeeze back through the hole."

"Into Penelope's garden," added Natty.

They peeped out just as Dad's boots approached and disappeared above them into the shed. His feet on the planks were deafening so it was a relief when he clomped outside again.

"He's going to dig up the carrots," said Natty, recognizing the garden fork, its prongs as thick as planks, fly above their heads.

"Let's go," said Ned. "The hole's at the bottom of the garden."

He trotted on to the path while Natty kept a lookout for big feet. They cantered to the safety of the rhubarb and paused. A quick glance under the umbrella leaves told them Flopper wasn't there.

Back on the path, Ned set off at a trot but was soon galloping so fast that the wind whistled. It was miles to the bottom of the garden and Natty held on tight.

They were tearing along at a terrific rate, when a missile the size of a tree trunk hurtled from the sky and landed in front of them. Natty ducked while Ned changed pace and jumped it. Another and another fell in quick succession, one behind them and one in front. Ned jumped the one in front, unbalancing Natty, who clung on until the end of the path where they took shelter under some spinach leaves.

"Someone's dropping trees," she said, thoroughly alarmed. Ned got his breath back as another orange missile joined the others on the path.

"Not trees – carrots," he said. "Pity there's no time for a nibble!"

He swung round and trotted on towards the hedge.

In front of them a square wooden structure grew high as a skyscraper. Natty knew it to be Dad's compost bin, full of grass cuttings and vegetable waste. Along the front, at ground level, was a place where one of the wooden slats had rotted, making a hole. Natty noticed it at once because poking from it, testing the air, was a pink nose.

"Look," she whispered. Ned froze into stillness. They watched as a white head emerged, a white head with a pair of floppy ears. "It's him." The rabbit blinked sleepy eyes.

"Well who'd have thought of looking in the compost heap," whispered Ned.

At which point footsteps thumped towards them. Ned quickly retreated into a jungle of spinach leaves. The startled Flopper reversed into his secret den just before black-booted legs stopped at the bin.

Above them, Dad threw a fistful of chewed pea pods on to the heap and raised the garden fork. It flashed down, biting into the earth in front of Flopper's hole. The footsteps clumped away again but the fork stayed put. Flopper was behind bars.

"Dad's trapped him," said Natty. "Without even knowing it."

"And a jolly good thing too," replied Ned. "All we need to do now is get you big again and you can collect him whenever you like."

Natty was overcome with delight. Flopper was found. She could hardly wait to tell Daisy.

But Flopper had no intention of remaining a prisoner. He urgently wanted to get out. He sniffed the prongs and tested all the gaps with his whiskers, but it was obvious he was too large to squeeze between any of them. With surprising determination he scrabbled against a prong with his front paws, and when nothing happened, returned into the hole.

"He's caught all right," said Ned.

But when Flopper reappeared bottom first and heaved against the prongs with his back, Natty wondered if Ned was mistaken. At first nothing happened, then slowly the fork toppled.

"Look out!" cried Natty.

As quick as a flash, Ned jumped sideways and for the second time that day Natty ended halfway up his neck.

The fork boinged to the ground beside them. Flopper gave a satisfied twitch of his whiskers and hopped from his hiding place. He tested the air once more and set off purposefully in the direction of the cabbages.

"That rabbit's going back for pudding," said Ned.

"I don't suppose he's ever heard of an angry gardener," said Natty, hauling herself back into the saddle. "We'd better get after him and quick before he eats something else."

Chapter 5

The Magician's Hat

Natty had never been frightened of a rabbit before, but then she had never met one five times bigger than she was, at least the size of a rhinoceros. As Ned closed the gap between them, the hopping rabbit appeared to grow larger. Natty couldn't think how to stop him.

"We must get you back to your proper size to catch Flopper," said Ned. "We'll go behind the runner beans. Hold tight."

Ned cantered for the cover of the beans and pulled up, blowing.

"Time to get off," he said.

"What will you do?"

"I'll go back to my picture. You catch that rabbit before he gets into more trouble."

Natty swung herself to the ground.

"Thank you for everything, Ned. Will you keep my riding clothes safe?"

"Of course," said Ned. "There's lots

more riding to come. Now go and catch that bunny."

Natty gave Ned a brief hug.

"Goodbye," she said, and let go of the reins. At once the wind bore her away. When she opened her eyes she was her proper size again and Ned had disappeared.

She peeped round the runner beans. Jamie was piling the carrots into a polythene bag. Flopper was inspecting a young cabbage plant and Dad was checking the remaining lettuces. Fortunately, he didn't know there were only the peas between himself and the greedy rabbit thief.

Voices and the sound of the side gate opening distracted everyone, even Flopper. It was Penelope Potter and her cousin Daisy. Penelope looked fed up and Daisy not far from tears. The two girls crossed the grass, stepping round Jamie's magician's hat and cloak which lay in a neglected heap.

A wonderful plan popped into Natty's head. She darted forward, scooped up the surprised rabbit before he took a single bite and, hugging her prize, darted back to her hiding place behind the runner beans. Amazingly, no one noticed.

"Hello, Penelope," said Jamie. "Who's your friend?"

"My cousin, Daisy."

"Hello," said Daisy.

"Isn't Natty with you?" asked Jamie. "We thought you were off riding Pebbles."

"Some chance! No, we're not riding Pebbles and we haven't seen Natty for ages," said Penelope, sniffily. Daisy pulled anxiously at the thin red lead she was carrying.

"We've been looking everywhere for Flopper," she said. Dad straightened up.

"And who may I ask is Flopper?"

"My pet rabbit."

"Your pet what!"

Daisy looked up with wide, startled eyes. It was an awkward moment, saved by Natty who jumped out from her hiding place.

"Hello, Penelope. Hi, Daisy."

"Natty, where've you been?" asked Dad.

"Looking for Flopper." For some reason she was no longer wearing her sweatshirt.

"I keep telling Daisy it's pointless,"

said Penelope. "If we haven't found him by now the fox is bound to have eaten him. They love rabbits, especially juicy ones who are too fat to run away."

Daisy's face crumpled and she took in a deep breath.

"NO!" she wailed. "STOP SAYING that!"

The noise brought Mum hurrying to find out what was wrong and everyone gathered around the unhappy little girl.

"Oh, Daisy, do shut up," said Penelope, embarrassed by all the fuss. "You've got to face facts. We can't find him and that's probably why."

In this noisy confusion Natty reached behind the beans and gently lifted a bundle from the ground before scampering across the grass to collect Jamie's magician's hat and cloak. Hands full, she hurried to the shed and scampered inside. Then she poked her head round the door and shouted above the din.

"Jamie! Come here a minute."

Daisy's cries lessened and everyone turned to look.

"What for?"

"Something peculiar's happened to your magician's hat." Jamie turned to the place where he had last seen it. The fact that it was gone sent him racing.

"What's happened to it?"

"This," said Natty, and pulled him into the shed and closed the door.

From inside came a lot of whispering.

Dad looked at Mum and raised an eyebrow.

He started towards the shed, but was stopped in his tracks when the door burst open and Natty jumped out, tootling a fanfare.

"Taa taddle, ta, ta, taddle, ta, taaaaaa! Ladies and gentlemen. Roll up, roll up, to see the great magician Jamie and his magic hat." Natty clapped for all she was worth. The audience looked surprised, and in Daisy's case, astonished.

With a swirl and a flourish, Jamie stepped from the shed. From under the black cloak he took out his magician's hat and his magic wand.

"Abracadabra, dee diddle dabbit." He waved the wand and tossed it to Natty.

"From out of my magic hat comes. . .

. . .A WHITE RABBIT!"

Triumphant, he lifted out one bemused white bunny. In the pause that followed, Daisy's expression changed from misery to joy.

"FLOPPER!" she gasped and rushed forwards.

Jamie placed the rabbit in her outstretched arms and the little girl nuzzled her face in his fur, covering him with her curls.

"Well blow me down," said Dad. "The thief in the garden, I presume!"

"Thank goodness for that," said Penelope. "Now we can go riding at last." She beamed at Jamie. "It was awfully clever of you to find him."

"I didn't," said Jamie. "It was Natty. I just did the thing I always wanted to do, pull a rabbit out of my hat. Brilliant!"

Later, when all the excitement had died down and Daisy had introduced Flopper to everyone, even Dad, Natty climbed the stairs to her bedroom. The first thing she saw was Tabitha, still fast asleep on the duvet. She turned to the

poster on the wall. Ned gazed out
in the direction of the window,
without doubt a picture pony
again. Natty ran her fingers over
the shiny paper and hoped no one
would notice that he was not in
quite the same position as before.

She lay on the bed and put her arms around Tabitha, stroking the cat's soft nose and fluffy head. Tabitha half opened her eyes and purred.

"I've had an amazing adventure," Natty whispered.

Then she smiled up at Ned. "And I wish more than anything for another one soon!"

The End